C000065032

ALL HALLOWS IN MIDDLEHAM

A STORY OF RICHARD III AND HIS SON EDWARD

BY J.P. Reedman

The soft, falling leaves pattered, red as blood, orange as a harvest moon, through the dales, over the hilltops, down through Coverdale where the monks sang in the choir of their secluded abbey. They made small, curl-prowed boats that sailed upon the wavelets of the Ure, coiling and swirling on the stygian waters of Black Dub, a bathing hole frequented by local youths in summer. But once autumn came, it was out of bounds: a dark place, home only to the chill-tinged wind and the dead and dying leaves.

A well-worn path from the Dub led over rising swells of land to the grey bulk of Middleham Castle. The leaves danced their autumnal waltz there too, floating over crenels, sweeping into the bailey, twining with the sinuous ripples of the huge banner that flapped, proudest of all, from the turret of the gatehouse. Duke Richard's banner, with its fierce White Boar emblem, the beast's tusks thrusting at the clouds hurrying overhead…

October was dying, along with the leaves, and winter would soon storm in with harsh and heavy tread, as it ever did in northern England, filling the dips and cups of the dales with white mantles of snow.

Edward of Middleham, the young son of Duke Richard, watched the leaves play as he walked through the castle bailey after visiting his favourite hawk in the mews. He eyed the puffy scuds of clouds overhead with suspicion and dislike. He did not enjoy the cold season. When the air was too cold, he coughed as gasped for air, and his nurses kept him shut indoors in the castle nursery. Yes, they told him stories, brought him sweetmeats and toy soldiers and such, and his father's big hounds were permitted in to lie on his feet and give extra warmth to his frozen toes, but it was hard to always dwell indoors so much, when other boys from the town were gambolling in the snow, hitting each other with snowballs and skating on the frozen surfaces of the Ure. Skating! Even had he not been prone to chesty coughs each winter, as his Lord Father's only legitimate son, he would never be permitted to bind animal shin-bones to his feet and skate on the ice!

He sighed deeply, imagining himself gliding across the river on those makeshift skates, as big and strong as any of the lads from the village…

"You look sad, little lord, if I may say so."

Edward glanced over to where old Gatty, the eldest of the castle's laundresses, was hauling in a huge woven basket of unwashed garments with a strength that belied her small statue and age. Her arms were bony but strong, the blue veins massed upon them like corded blue ropes. She had few teeth and what was left of her hair was hidden under a white linen cap, but her smile was full of warmth. She was known in the town as a great storyteller, and her daughter Aileth was a herbalist—Edward's mother, Duchess Anne, used her services to get poultices and tissanes when Edward suffered his winter maladies.

"I am not sad," he said, "but winter is on its way. Other than our Lord's birthday, which isn't celebrated for two more months, it is very dull. If it gets too cold, it means I cannot go outside, and if the streets get blocked by snow, no one can visit the castle either…"

"It's a pity you cannot go soul-caking with the little 'uns down the town," Gatty said with a heartfelt sigh. "But that's not for small lordlings in the making, alas." She heaved her basket onto her hip with a grunt. "Now I must be on my way, Master Edward, else your Lady Mother won't have her clear linens and she won't be best pleased."

Edward waved the old woman farewell and watched as she trudged across the bailey to the timber-walled hut where the laundresses worked, trampling the cloth in huge wooden tubs constantly refilled with boiled water, with added mixtures of ash and urine. "It's a hard job," he had once heard Gatty say to her fellows, "but at least me feet are always clean—the feet of a fifteen-year-old they are, though on the body of a sixty-year-old!"

Edward had wanted to ask the laundress more about the 'soul caking' she had mentioned but knew better than to hold her from her tasks, since all chores in the castle had to be completed on time in order for life to run smoothly. The steward might see him and chide him, or one of his tutors…or worse, Father, who had not long arrived back in Middleham, after dealing with the Scots on King Edward's orders.

He chewed on his lower lip, a habit he had inherited from his father when contemplative or worried. Father knew of all that happened within Middleham, but it was too soon to pester the Duke with any questions—he was resting from his long journey home. The cold and long days in the saddle caused him grievous pain in his back and he would sit alone with his physician, who would place heated stones and liniments upon the sore areas. So Edward decided the best bet would be to see his mother, Anne, instead.

The Duchess of Gloucester was in her comfortable and cosy solar, its walls painted in bright swathes of red and green and trimmed with gilding. A statue of the Virgin and Child, crafted from Nottingham alabaster, smiled benignly from a niche in the wall, a candle burning at the Virgin's feet; there were screens for dressing in private, painted with scenes of hunts or strutting peacocks with their jewelled plumage spread in gaudy array. There was a large bed, furnished with rich, silk hangings and embroidered with the symbols of the Duchess's paternal family, the Earls of Warwick.

Mother herself was sitting in the window embrasure with three of her ladies, including her half-sister Margaret, who was a few years older and baseborn. Edward liked his Aunt Margaret; she was kind and quick-witted, and recently she had brought him a small bow to play with. Despite being illegitimate, Margaret was firmly part of the family, as were Edward's own baseborn half-brother and sister, John and Katherine. Most of the time these two children lived at Father's other great stronghold at Sheriff Hutton but sometimes they came to Middleham to visit. Katherine was here now, for Mother and Aunt Margaret were teaching her dance and the arts appropriate for girls. She had tutors at Sheriff Hutton, of course, but Father liked to check on her progress himself, and he also thought it a good idea for her to have some highborn female company...

"Greetings, little Edward." Margaret put down her stitchery and smiled at her nephew. "Did you visit your favourite hawk?"

"Yes, Aunt, his name is Achilles," said Edward, nodding enthusiastically. "He's a type of peregrine and is Father's favourite too. I also went to the kennels. The grey bitch, Mist, has had a litter of puppies—four of them. The kennel master let me hold them."

"So a good day then, Edward," said Margaret.

"Yes, it was, but…" He tilted his head, hesitating.

"But what, Edward?" said his mother. "I can tell something is bothering you. I always know such things."

"Mother, what is 'soul caking?' Old Gatty mentioned it."

"Ah," said Anne. "The children do it every year. They go from door to door in the town on All Hallows and All Souls, asking for alms and Soul Cakes, which are little buns made with dried fruits and cinnamon or ginger."

Edward's eyes grew round at the description of the cakes. Like many young boys, he had a taste for sweet things, although he was as thin as a whipcord.

Aunt Margaret cleared her throat, hiding a smile. "Those cakes are not meant to merely fill the bellies of hungry little boys. Each cake represents the soul of one who has passed away. One who is now in Purgatory, waiting for release. The Souler asking for the cake must solemnly promise to say many prayers to release the souls of the dead from their long wait."

Edward's gaze swivelled to his mother. "C-can I go and watch?" he asked shyly. And then, taking a deep breath and drawing himself up as proudly as he could, he said, "I could show my half-sister Katherine. I would protect her when we were out in the dark and keep her from being afraid."

Anne's brow furrowed. "I must ask your father. We have never taken you into the town on All Hallows Night before, for we deemed you too young. Indeed, your sire may well *still* decide you are too young. But I will ask him as I can see it means something to you. If he grants his permission, you will go suitably accompanied—don't imagine for one second you will be out alone or knocking on doors…" Anne leaned forward, putting her hands on Edward's thin shoulders and looking straight into his dark blue-grey eyes, so similar to Duke Richard's. "Why are you so interested in All Hallows and All Souls? Tell me, child? Something is bothering you; I know as a mother always does."

Edward took another deep breath. "Winter. All Hallows heralds winter. And once winter comes I cannot go out till the warmer days of spring…"

Anne and Margaret glanced at each other, both a little sorrowful. "Your father the Duke and have explained to you why, Edward," said Anne in a soft voice. "You know what the physician told us. If you did not understand why, I could have him come to remind you…."

"I know I must take care." Edward refused to meet her gaze and swallowed deeply as if on the verge of tears. "I am my father's only legitimate son and heir…and I am *delicate*…" He said the last word as if it were poison, burning his tongue. "That means I must avoid the cold, the night air…" His lip began to tremble but then he flushed red and became somewhat mutinous. "It isn't *fair,* Lady Mother! And people will laugh at me! What noble's son must forever lurk inside with the milkmaids and nursemaids? Will the men of the north ever follow me when I am older? Or do they pray that you will have another son that will supplant me while I am sent to a monastery?"

Anne gasped. She was very surprised her son, only six, spoke with such impassioned words. She had thought he didn't realise his frailty and was happy enough to play with the dogs and pore over the illuminated books in Duke Richard's library. She should have known better. Edward was small in body but he had the intellect of an older boy…and with no full-blooded brothers or sisters living at Middleham, much time to ponder on what his physician had told his parents.

"Edward," Anne cried, "you must never think so. You must take care now, in your extreme youth…but your father and I have been assured that you will grow out of your childhood ailments. Your own father was small and deemed sickly as a boy…and look at him now, riding around the whole of the North Country and even to Scotland, and fighting in battles. You must be patient; you know that is a noble virtue."

Margaret touched her sister's arm, drawing her away from her son, who still looked unhappy, his mouth downturned and his hands knotted into tight balls. "Anne, it is not my place to interfere…but I think my nephew speaks some truth. Do not be angry with me—but you and Richard cannot keep him wrapped in soft lambswool forever. Let him go into Middleham with Katherine and some attendants for company. Look at the longing on his face! It would make him so happy and give him confidence."

"I know you speak truth," murmured Anne, and tears dampened her eyes for a moment, "but it worries me so. One year he was so poorly he could barely breathe…If anything should happen to him…"

"I understand your fear," said Margaret, "but think of him, and what his future will be someday. Think of his own happiness. You must put your faith in God where Edward is concerned. Anne. He is not some frail canary to languish within a cage until deemed strong enough to fly."

Anne sighed, and leaving Margaret, walked over to Edward. "You have heard what your aunt thinks. Perhaps she is right. I must confer with your father before any decision is made. I can promise you nothing, though."

"Oh, thank you, Mother!" cried Edward, and he raced forward and flung his arms around her waist. Then he whirled around and ran from the solar, grinning from ear to ear with joy.

"You have done the right thing, Anne," said Margaret, patting her half-sister's arm.

"I hope so," said the Duchess with a sigh. "Now I must go and approach Richard. I have no idea how he will react. Part of me wishes he would forbid it...but then I think of the smile on Edward's face and how I would not gladly see it replaced by disappointed tears."

Duchess Anne went to find her husband. He was relaxing in his own apartments, a goblet of malmsey in his hand, one foot upon a padded stool. Two hounds lay at his feet, basking in the warmth of the flames in the fireplace. His illegitimate daughter Katherine sat at his feet, a slender, fine-boned willowy girl a few years older than Edward, with curled dark hair and pale skin; she was showing him her accomplishments in reading as she read aloud from a thick, leather-bound tome.

As Anne entered the chamber, she leapt up, curtseying respectfully. "I will go to my chamber now…if that is your wish, my Lady," she said.

"No, stay, Katherine," said Anne, gesturing for Katherine to sit once more. "What I am about to discuss with your Lord Father involves you too."

Katherine sat back down on her cushion and Richard beckoned Anne into another carved chair standing near the fire. "What is it that troubles you, Anne?"

"What makes you think I am troubled?" she replied with a wan smile.

"I know you well enough to tell when you are ill at ease," said Richard. "Speak and I will see if I can ease whatever distresses you."

"It's Edward…" began Anne.

"My brother or my son?"

"Our Edward. Our little Ned…"

Richard tensed slightly and leaned forward in his chair. "Our Ned…he is well?" He trailed off, hands splayed on his knees, his eyes locked on his wife's face.

"Yes, yes, he's well…never better," Anne said hurriedly, trying not to alarm him. "In fact, he is so well…that he is begging me to let him watch the Souling begin on All Hallows Eve. He wants to go with

Katherine…as her protector." She couldn't help but flash an honest, amused smile at the thought. Her boy…already the chivalrous knight.

"Oh!" Katherine cried, clapping her hands together in delight. "I would LOVE that! Can we go, Father? Can we?"

"That was what worried you, Anne?" Richard blinked at his wife. "Ned wanting to see the Souling?".

"Yes, you know why…his weak chest."

"We'll make certain he is wrapped up warm. If I had known he was interested in such a thing, I would have given my permission already. Yes, he may go into Middleham tomorrow night, with Katherine…and we will accompany him too. It always heartens the townsfolk when we walk amongst them, and it behoves us to make ourselves accessible to them."

Edward gave an excited squeal and rushed to clasp his half-sister's hands and pull her to her feet, jumping around in excitement like a new puppy. Katherine tried to keep some shred of decorum but his mood was infectious and she began to laugh as he spun her around the chamber.

"So much happiness," said Margaret, appearing in the doorway. "Sister, they will not forget their first All Hallows and All Souls…It will bring much excitement, never to be forgotten. Far better than having no memories, or only an unpleasant memory of being told 'No'."

Dusk arrived early at the dead-end of October, the sky turning purplish then blue-black as the sun slipped behind the hills. A round orange moon rode the heavens between banks of clouds streaming from the west. There was no ground fog, save for a few stray vapours coiling off the Ure, but the air was hazy with smoke from numerous bonfires lit around the town and up the dale sides, making ghosts of living men and cloaking the streets, marketplace, and the crenellated tower of St Alkelda's church with grey. The scent of burning leaves and old dry animal bones washed over Middleham, a scent both earthy and vaguely sinister.

The Duke and Duchess exited the castle with the children, both of whom were wrapped in rich fur cloaks with the hoods up to ward off the chill. A small entourage followed them, shadowy figures in the moving smoke.

As they walked, the bells from the church tower began to toll—an endless metallic clangour. They were joined by bells from the castle chapel and, more distantly, the bells from Coverdale Abbey and Jervaulx. Out from cottages and byres came the townsfolk of Middleham, children dressed in their best, carrying turnip lanterns in their hands or mounted on sticks. The hollowed turnips bobbed like disembodied heads in the gloom, their gnarled, wizened faces spilling ghoulish candlelight from slashed-out triangle eyes and grinning mouths.

Edward gasped at the sight of them and grasped Katherine's hand; she looked a little frightened too but also full of anticipation. "Let's follow the procession!" she said breathlessly, gesturing to the backs of the village children, who were now forming a rather disorderly parade, winding around the market square with the turnip lanterns floating before them, eerie under the globe of the half-cowled moon.

Duke Richard nodded his agreement to his daughter's wishes and the little party from the castle set off to join the townsfolk gathering in the square. It was not unusual to see the Duke or his Lady out in the town, but unusual on a night like this, when they usually remained within the castle, praying in the chapel and having candles lit for their dead ancestors and family members. Local women curtseyed, old and young, some with faded autumn leaves twined in their hair or a necklace of threaded nuts; men bowed with respect—the butcher, the candle, the baker, the smith and others, one or two masked like mummers. The town's children coiled away shyly, clutching their grinning turnip lanterns close, not so used to seeing nobility close up as their elders. Katherine and Edward trailed in the wake of the Duke and Duchess, wide-eyed, savouring the strange sights and sounds.

Up ahead, some of the children were knocking on doors, calling out they had come to offer prayers for the family's dead. Women emerged bearing platters of the Souling cakes, marked with a cross or topped by dried fruit, some still hot from the oven and sending off tendrils of steam into the increasingly chilly night.

Edward took a deep breath. "They smell good," he said wistfully.

Duke Richard gestured with a nod of his head to one of his personal attendants. The man went to one of the nearby cottages, a turnip-lap fluttering on the doorstep, and spoke briefly to the residents before handing over a small jingling bag to the goodwife. A few minutes later, the servant returned to the ducal party with several Soul Cakes wrapped in a linen kerchief which he handed to Duke Richard with a bow.

Richard took the kerchief carefully and opened it before Edward and Katherine's hungry gaze. "One cake for each of you," he said, adding with mock sternness: "But you must promise that you will say prayers before bed tonight for all the souls of those who have lived and died in Middleham."

"We will, we promise!" the two children clamoured, reaching for the still-hot cakes.

"Eat them carefully," chided Duchess Anne, peering over. "You do not want to burn your mouths."

The cakes devoured, the little party headed towards the church of Saint Alkelda, where the church bells were tolling ever onwards, as they would all night, filling the air with their strident peels. The normally dark churchyard was tonight filled with the flutter of torches and the tapers inside hollowed turnips as people of all ages came to pray for relatives long buried in that hallowed ground. Despite the association with the dead, the mood was not sombre but merry and full of excitement. Some youngsters danced around a bare-branched tree growing at the back of the church, some with faces disguised by a dash of ash-paint or chalk. By the half-overgrown well of St Alkelda, village maidens sat combing out their hair, vain as mermaids, giggling as they peeled apples and threw the peel onto the ground, imagining that they could divine who they might marry from the shapes formed by the fallen apple skin.

The church had existed in Middleham for at least a hundred years, though locals said it stood upon an ancient Saxon shrine to Saint Alkelda, a pious princess who had been martyred by pagan Norse women when she would not recant her faith, typing a scarf around her throat and drawing it tight. Recently King Edward had granted his brother, the Duke, to make Saint Alkelda's a collegiate church, in honour of Christ, His Mother the Blessed Virgin, and Saint

Alkelda. It had priests and choristers and a small, new chantry chapel where the Duke and Duchess could pray for the souls of their departed ancestors and for the wellbeing of their living ones, especially the King and his heirs.

Richard and Anne entered the church nave with the children, while the rest of their party remained outside with the revellers in the churchyard. Hushed, they proceeded to the private chantry chapel, blazing with candlelight, the air muggy with the fragrance of tallow, beeswax and incense. After they had all prayed for various great personages— King Edward, Queen Elizabeth, the little princes and princesses, and the respected dead, including the Duke's father, Richard Duke of York, his brother Edmund, both slain at Wakefield and Anne's father, the famous Richard Neville, Earl of Warwick, who fell at Barnet...unfortunately fighting on the 'wrong' side. Richard also prayed for his brother George, executed by the King a few years back, an act that caused him great grief—and a lack of desire to fare to London and the royal court unless summoned.

Once these important prayers were complete, the Duke, Duchess and children returned to the churchyard, which was even more crowded than before. A bagpipe wheezed; a viol shrilled. The moon emerged fully from a patch of clouds and lit up tombs and the church's stalwart walls, bathing them in a shivering silver-blue light.

Edward caught sight of old Gatty, the castle laundress, sitting beneath the boughs of a yew, that tree known as the guardian of the graveyard for its long life and the sap that ran red if the trunk were breached, just like a man's life-blood.

Gatty looked quite different without the simple apron and white cap she wore while washing garments and bed linens at the castle laundry. Now she wore a proper matron's wimple and a woollen gown dyed a dark blue with a short tunic over it. Her face was less red than when she was trampling and beating soiled clothes and pouring bucketloads of boiled water on them.

"Gatty!" Ned cried, delighted, and without thinking, he ran towards her.

Gatty looked alarmed as the little boy approached, or rather, she was alarmed to see his highborn parents following close on his heels. Gatty herself was already surrounded by the town's children, their mouths flecked by soul-cake crumbs. She struggled to her feet, brushing down her skirts and curtseyed to the Duke and Duchess of Gloucester. "Your Graces, I did not expect to see you here tonight…"

"Seat yourself, mistress," said Richard with a smile. "We are not here to chide you. What is it you do on this holy eve?"

She looked down, embarrassed. "Telling the old tales, my Lord. Silly old stories from long ago…"

"About ghosts and witches!" shouted out a young child, who seemed not to be frightened by this at all, but rather jubilant.

Gatty's cheeks now flushed crimson, redder than when she worked in the laundry amidst the steam. "Oh, my lord, I hope you won't be thinkin' ill of me for telling such tales. It's a tradition here, on this night, though no doubt not amongst fine folk like yourselves."

"Oh, I would not be so sure of that," said Richard. "When I was a lad, I remember my old nurse telling me the legend of Snowball the Tailor, who was knocked off his horse by a sinister raven that turns out to be a restless spirit…. My mother never objected as far as I know and other than a few sleepless nights, I was unharmed!"

"I have your permission to continue then, your Grace?" The relief on Gatty's face was palpable.

"Of course!" said Richard, seemingly surprised that she would even ask.

"Can we stay, Father?" asked Edward, reaching up to touch the end of the Duke's crimson velvet sleeve. "Please?"

Richard frowned and rubbed his chin, pretending to consider the matter with great gravity. "Hmm, I do not know if you are yet old enough."

"I am!" cried Edward, drawing himself up to his full height and puffing out his chest, despite Katherine's muffled titters. "I won't be scared of *anything*...just like you. I promise, Lord Father."

"Very well, then," said Richard, suppressing a grin behind a gloved hand. "You may stay...and protect Katherine."

"I don't need..." Katherine began to retort; she was at that age that even though she dearly loved her little half-brother, she did not want to appear as if were frail and weak. Indeed, although she was slight and small herself, she was agile and a swift runner; she looked pretty and feminine in hennin and gown, dancing to courtly airs...but behind her nursemaids' backs, she was often found shimmying up apple trees, gallivanting with hounds or currying ponies in the stables.

Anne gave the girl a wry little look. "I am sure you will be most grateful for the protection of Edward's sword arm..."

"But he doesn't have a..." began Katherine, and then she realised that the Duchess was telling her, without speaking the obvious, to humour her small brother and not hurt his feelings.

"Oh, yes, of course," she said, giving her father and Anne a knowing look. "He can sit by me and hold my hand in case I become frightened."

The two children hurried over to Gatty's side and sat on the grass near the tatty hem of her voluminous skirts. The town children backed away, in awe of these noble newcomers. They soon lost their fear, however, and began to point in wonder at Edward and Katherine's velvet clothing and the gold buckles gleaming on their shoes.

Gatty cleared her throat nervously, all too aware of the presence of the Duke and

Duchess of Gloucester, who had retreated behind a worn grave marker to make themselves unobtrusive. Despite their best efforts, though, a jewel winked on the brim of Richard's hat and a blue sapphire sparkled like a fallen star on a necklace around Anne's slender throat.

However, like a true thespian, Gatty ploughed on, sweeping an arm toward the sea of rapt faces around her, drawing them all closer. "You've all ridden horses around Middleham, haven't you?" she said, gazing from one child's face to the next. "Well, I give you good warning—if you are out playing by the river, do not try to mount any horses or ponies that come trotting along, even if they snuffle at your neck or bow their heads before you, imploring you to mount. The reason is…no matter how appealing they seem, they are not *real* horses."

"What are they then?" piped a lad of about twelve who sported a ginger block of clumsily cut hair. He was the local miller's boy, known for flaming hair and flaming temper.

"Monsters!" said Gatty in a hushed voice, her eyes narrowing to slits.

A murmur went through the children in the churchyard.

"Yes, monsters," the old storyteller continued, leaning forward, her hands splayed on her knees. "They are Water Horses, not true horses at all. If you get close enough, you will see green weeds braided in their manes and tails, and their eyes shine red as blood. Should one rear on its hinds, you would notice webbing across the frog of its hoof. But you wouldn't want to get that close…because if you did, you'd most likely never see home again!"

Another murmur from the gathered children, even more uneasy than the last. Edward wriggled closer to Katherine.

"You see…" Gatty licked her lips. The flickering lights from the candles and torches lighting the churchyard made her face resemble the turnip lanterns carried by Middleham's younglings. "Water Horses don't eat grass and straw. They crave one delicacy only…fresh human livers."

She made a smacking noise with her nigh-toothless mouth and her audience screeched, half with terror, half with delight. "Our very own Water Horse sleeps in the weeds below the surface of Black Dub, down past the castle and over the rise," she went on.

"I used to swim there with Lovell and Percy when I was a lad." Duke's Richard's disembodied voice wafted out of the shadows, making everyone jump.

"Then, my Lord Duke, you're a very lucky man," said Gatty, fighting back a grin to look very serious indeed. "The Water Horse was surely hiding at the bottom of the Dub when you were there, grinding his teeth as he thought how tasty royal flesh might be…though perhaps he was afraid of taking on anyone descended from such a valorous lineage. My goodness, if he'd known such a beast was lurking about, holding evil designs on his young brother, no doubt King Edward would have ridden up here in a trice and cut off the beast's evil head."

"No doubt at all," laughed Richard. He leaned against the ancient tombstone, the warm light of a passing torch catching on his jewellery, making the red gem in his ring glow like blood. "I would have attempted to give the beast a good thrashing myself too, small though I was!"

Gatty smiled and returned to her story. "Our wicked Water Horse is not the only one living in these dales, either, children. There's another one, even bit as evil and malicious, over by Bolton Abbey, on a section of the river known as The Strid. It rises from the foam and spray of the river, sometimes taking on the shape of a beautiful woman or handsome man. This deception makes it even more dangerous than its fellow at Middleham."

"What…what can we do to keep safe from these dreadful horses?" asked a young girl, her freckled face tense in the uncertain light. She twiddled nervously with one of her long, tawny braids.

"Don't go to the Dub or anywhere along the riverbanks alone," said Gatty, nodding wisely. "Always take someone with you. And if you must swim in summertime, beware of the reeds and weeds…for the Horse likes to hide there, watching for the unwary. Be careful too in winter, my young dears, for if you go skating alone and fall through the ice, he'll drag you down, and you'll strike the ice above with your fists, even as bubbles come from your mouth…"

She paused, glancing toward the Duke and Duchess of Gloucester. "My apologies, your Graces, if that was a bit strong. I was probably getting sommat carried away, spooking these children so."

Richard gave a shrug. "Cautionary tales can have great value if they teach the young to take care when they are out alone."

Gatty took a sip of ale from the horn jug propped up at her side. "Well, enough of Water Horses. How do you little 'uns feel about…*witches*?"

"I heard the priest say that witchcraft ain't real!" cried one of the older youths gathered amongst the tombs.

"They burn 'em!" shouted someone else, almost gleefully.

"Nah," another youth of about fourteen retorted. "That ain't right, Matthew. Mostly they hang witches, witches are hanged…don't you know nothin'?"

Gatty held up a hand for silence. "Well, the witch I'm going to tell you about isn't that kind of a witch. Not practicing black sorcery or trying to set evil spells on the King and his family. The witch in my tale is not human, she is one of the faerie folk—who some say were minor fallen angels, others the spirits of unbaptised pagans of yore—you know, deemed too good for hell, but too bad for heaven. Her name is Churn Milk Peg…but it ain't butter she churns. She guards nuts on the trees when children try to pick them afore they are ripe. When the nuts are pulpy is when they are called 'churn-milk' and it's also the favourite time for little 'uns to try to pick 'em."

"What does this Peg do?" breathed Katherine. "I—I picked some nuts off a bush once."

"You were very lucky, little mistress," said Gatty, waggling a finger. "By any chance, did you see a great tall stone standing nearby?"

"I-I cannot remember."

"Well, any big standing stone near a hazelnut tree is probably Peg, spying on you and deciding if she feels like showing herself… and maybe going on the attack!"

"Does this hag eat you like the Water Horse?" chortled a dubious older boy his shoulders already broad from work in the fields beside his father. "I'd give her a clout if she came at me!"

Gatty's lips pursed. "She might look like a feeble old woman, Will Underhill…till you see her iron teeth and serpent's eyes! She carries a long wooden pipe, and as she approaches the thieving childer, she sings,

Sing, sing, my wooden pipe, they're gathering the nuts ere they're ripe! She then puts the pipe to her lips and plays an eerie song, a song of earth and stone, fire and ice, and with that, her victims are stuck to the ground, unable to move, their hands full of the pilfered milk-churn nuts. Her wickedness done, Peg herds her prisoners away, to take them to the Owd Lad, and you know who that is, don't you?" She peered about her, with eyebrows raised.

No one answered, they all seemed too afraid to speak. Even the youths were silent, glancing nervously at each other.

"He's the one also known as Owd Nick. Satan…the devil himself," said Gatty in a rush, staring up as if she feared that Beezelbub would swoop above her from above and carry her off. But there was nought above save the hurrying clouds and a few bats that soared soundlessly between the church tower and the yew tree.

Nonetheless, a hush had fallen over the crowd; it was bad luck to speak of the Evil One, especially on a night like tonight—for though All Hallows was a night to chant Christian prayers for the deceased and those confined in purgatory, it was also a night when folk said the souls of the unforgiven dead would roam—revenants of murderers, suicides buried at the crossroads, the babes who were not baptised and laid in unhallowed ground beyond the churchyard's stone wall…

Gatty broke the silence. "But no one here's been stealing unripe nuts recently, have they?"

A chorus of 'no's' sounded, quiet at first and then growing stronger. "I hope not," added Duke Richard. "To gather them so early just wastes them as they are barely edible."

"His Lordship speaks the truth." Gatty nodded. "If you won't listen to me, listen to his Grace."

She let out a deep breath; it foamed white before her mouth. The moon was westering and the night cooling off, even with the lit bonfires around town. A lacy haze of frost glimmered across the grass.

"It's growing late," said Gatty. "Soon you should all be in bed…'cos Father Gregory will expect you up early and in Mass tomorrow morn. But…if your eyes are not already closing in boredom—I will tell you one more tale this All Hallows Eve. What say you all!" She stifled a yawn with her work-roughened hand.

Immediately the children started crying out for more. Although many were indeed tired, their eyes bleary and stinging from the acrid bonfire smoke and their hair reeking of the pyre, it was exciting to be out so late with the adults and to face the perils of the restless dead on All Hallows Eve.

"Well, then…" Gatty slapped her thigh. "One more tale it is tonight! This one will be about an ancient giant who lived right here in Wensleydale. He dwelt in a strong, stone castle centuries before Alan Rufus built the first wooden fortress behind our present castle, back in the days of the Conqueror. The giant had blazing red hair and beard, and a temper to match; men whispered that he was descended from the old heathen god, Thor, who brought the thunder with strikes of his mighty hammer and rode in an airborne chariot drawn by the magical goats Tooth-barer and Tooth-grinder…|"

The younglings all laughed now, always amused by the myths of other people from a long-gone, distant past—somehow they seemed less frightening than the tales of boggarts, hobs and faerie folk that still dwelt, according to many, in lonely coppices, dells, stone circles and fosses.

"Anyway," Gatty leaned back, "the giant of Wensleydale, let's call him, Rombald, lived up on Penhill, after his mother, a Frost Giantess, dumped him there as an unwanted babe. Some of you may know the place; on a clear day, you can even see the hill from the battlements of our Lord Richard's castle. Rombald lived on his own save for his herd of prized pigs and a grizzled grey hound as big as a wolf which he, rather appropriately, called 'Wolfshead'."

"A Wolfshead is an outlaw!" cried one of the boys. "Like Robin Hood!"

Gatty nodded. "Yes, and Rombald and Wolfshead the Hound behaved like outlaws, too, stealing and killing animals...and local villagers. One day, when Rombald was rounding up his precious pigs, he noticed a flock of sheep running around the foot of Penhill. Filled with malice, he set Wolfshead upon them, who wreaked red ruin on the hapless sheep with fang and claw. The shepherdess who was herding the sheep, a fair maiden called Gunda, ran towards the giant, weeping as she begged him for mercy. 'Spare my animals, good Rombald! The sheep are my only livelihood! I will starve in the winter should they all be killed!' she cried. 'Well, I can make sure you never have to worry about starving again!' the beast sneered, and he struck her so hard with his iron-studded club she fell down instantly dead."

Katherine uttered a little scream, hastily muting the sound with her hand, so as not to appear weak before her young half-brother. Edward patted her on the shoulder comfortingly. In the gloom, their father crossed his arms and smiled to himself…when no one else could see.

"Rombald started to laugh at the wanton destruction he had wrought, but then he noticed something odd. Wolfshead, his one and only companion, stood growling at him, lips curled back and hackles raised. Enraged at his disloyalty, he lashed out and struck the hound with his club, even as he had struck poor helpless Gunda. So now Wolfshead lay still and dead beside the body of the unfortunate shepherdess, while Rombald, still fuming at his pet's betrayal, stomped up the rocky slopes to the castle atop Penhill."

"He was a very bad giant!" shrilled one of the smallest members of the audience, a curly-haired boy with remnants of the soul cakes making a moustache on his lip. "I hope a knight comes to punish him! To chop off his head!"

Duke Richard uttered a little laugh from his vantage point in the gloomy churchyard. "It is so interesting to watch how the youngest demand justice, even if it seems harsh. Older men...well, many judges are swayed by money or by the stature of he who they must pass sentence upon." Beside him, Anne nodded and reached out to surreptitiously take his hand in the dark.

Gatty glanced at the circle of faces around her, eyeing those particularly rapt, eager to hear of justice meted out on the killer. "Rombold didn't get away with his wickedness, I am glad to say. As the giant climbed up to his castle, an old man appeared out of the mist, his hair grey and shaggy, his brows bristling like hedges—and his eye was sapphire-blue and keen. I say *eye*, for he had but one, shining in the mirk of that sunless day. He bore a great oak staff topped by a ruby and wore a tall, conical hat topped by an eagle's feather. He was, as you may have already guessed, a wizard."

The audience began to clap noisily, guessing what was next to come.

"The old man stared at the two outstretched bodies on the ground, shaking his head in sorrow and anger. 'I knew that giant long ago,' he said, 'and he has lost his way. An end must be made, alas, and his spirit sent flying across the northern mountains and away to the end of the world.' He lifted his staff and crimson light streamed from it like blood, lighting Gunda's bloodless dead face and Wolfshead's ruffled fur. A moment later, a miracle happened—both began to breathe and their wounds vanished. Girl and dog scrambled to their feet, confused but very much alive. 'Arise, children, of both mortal and canine stock!" cried the one-eyed wizard, holding his staff aloft. "Go seek your revenge on he who cruelly laid you low!'"

"Gunda began to stride towards the grim fortress louring atop Penhill, with Wolfshead bounding on her heels. As they climbed the path to the summit of the hill, Gunda cried out for Rumbald to come out of hiding and atone for his crimes. Inside the castle, in a vast hall with a fire where the giant roasted both sheep and human beings before sucking marrow from their cracked bones, Rumbald heard the maid's voice with a start of fear. *The girl!* It could not be. His brow, craggy as a mountainside, lowered in a dreadful frown."

Gatty staggered up, making the most hideous face to emulate the giant's glowering countenance. "So…" she flung her bony arms wide, her sleeves flapping in the chill night breeze like a shroud, "Rumbald picked up his spiked club and marched out into the bailey, his steps so heavy they shook the ground below. Before the iron gate stood Gunda and Wolfshead, both seemingly returned from death and waiting for some kind of retribution."

Clapping and cheering came from the circle of children. "Kill 'im! Kill the giant!" some began to chant.

Gatty held up a hand for silence. A hush descended. "Rumbald's bloodshot eyes turned red as fire when he saw his victims returned from death. But there was fear in that malevolent gaze as well as rage; none of his previous victims—and there were hundreds!—had ever returned from the dead to confront him! He took a long stride forward, his bellows of wrath rolling around the dales like thunder and flung open the gate. He raised his club on high, seeking to strike down his tormentors for a second time—only this time he would shatter every bone in their bodies with his club and then grind the bones down to make his bread. There would be nothing left to return to life again. Gunda, who stood still as a stone with her hand on Wolfshead's ruff was unafraid. 'Go, stout-hearted dog!' she cried to the hound. 'The giant let *you* down most of all, who had served him all these years and was his only friend…' Wolfshead let out a growl that was closer to a bear's roar. Bristling, he bounded across the ground towards Rumbald. The giant swung at him with his weapon but Wolfshead sprang into the air, fangs bared, and sank his teeth into Rumbald's great, meaty neck. Blood spouted into the air…"

There were gasps from the younger children; one or two blocked their ears with their hands. Several of the older ones giggled, trying to show that they were not afraid like the little ones.

Gatty wiped her forehead with her sleeve as if the emotion of the fight was almost too much for her to bear. "Aye, it was a gory scene, but no matter how much Rumbald staggered about, beating at his one-time companion, he could not dislodge the dog or pry his jaws apart. The giant began to grow weak, his eyes blurring, turning in circles on the hilltop and swaying this way and that. Wolfshead latched on the tighter with his long, sharp fangs, and suddenly the two of them were teetering on the edge of Penhill where it backed over a steep slope, filled with broken boulders that stuck up like honed knives. Wolfshead's jaws opened and then snapped shut again with renewed fury, and with a scream that rent heaven and earth, Rumbald toppled backwards over the edge, the dog still savaging him as they fell together…."

"W-what happened then?" Edward spoke out now. He was quite sorry about the dog falling over the cliff as he liked playing with his father's hounds very much. And Katherine had a brachet called Noseworthy who would always unexpectedly stick his cold wet nose against your leg or hand while searching for treats. You would jump in alarm when you felt that nose snuffling at your skin…but then you'd laugh when he looked beseechingly at you with his big brown eyes.

Gatty sighed. "Realising that the giant was dead, the local folk stormed his castle and that very night set fire to it. It blazed against the sky for hours while the villagers danced in celebration of the death of the tyrant. He was surely dead, although it seemed his gross corpse had melted into the boulders on the hillside, forming a twisted lumpen mass of stones. Alas, Wolfshead the hound vanished with none knowing his fate…"

Edmund stared down, glum, wishing the dog had survived. But many stories had no happy ending; he was old enough to know that.

"What about the shepherdess, Gunda?" asked Katherine. Edward gave her a perturbed look and rolled his eyes—who cared about some silly sheep-herding girl when a *dog* was missing?

"The old grey wizard came for her and all the villagers bowed to him and said nought, for they could see she was changed and no longer one of them. So instead of returning to her flocks, Gunda went off with the wizard—to where no one knows. Maybe Wolfshead was unharmed and found his way to her side…Hmm, in fact, I am *certain* that is exactly what happened…." Gatty gave Edward a comforting little smile and he brightened up immediately at the thought that Wolfshead might have averted his doom.

The crowd of youngsters began to dissipate, the All Hallows storytelling over. Above the moon continued to sail into the West, growing faint and pale; the castle battlements were black, save for where the fire-braziers of the sentries burned. Smoke hung like mist about the churchyard and across the town of Middleham. People were beginning to seek their cottages now and the bonfires were burning to embers. Tomorrow would be All Hallows Day and the next day All Souls; there would be much prayer, and fond remembrance of the dead and...more Soul Cakes with their little crosses.

Edward got to his feet and moved close to his parents. He was not coughing but the night air had begun to make his chest feel tight, although he resolved to say nothing. Duchess Anne peered at her son through the gloom and frowned. "Richard, Ned looks very tired."

Richard nodded in agreement. He motioned to one of his attendants to carry the lad on his shoulders. If he had been a poor man, an ordinary man of the town, he would have carried Edward himself...but it was not fitting for a royal Duke to be seen in such a manner. "Now you are a giant!" the Duke said, gazing up to the child as he clung to the neck of a tall, burly Yorkshireman long in the service of the Nevilles before the Duke came to Middleham with Anne as his wife. "Jesu, you are even taller than your uncle the King right now!"

Richard then turned to Gatty who had wrapped her shawl around her shoulders and was readying to depart for the comforts of her cottage—her old lame husband who snored before the fire and her two cats, the Red Mouser and Tibbles with the white bib.

"My thanks for entertaining the children tonight," said the Duke, slipping a few coins into her hand. "And for changing the ending of the last tale to a happier one."

Gatty shrugged ruefully. "I couldn't help myself, your Grace. There are few enough happy endings in real life, are there? At least I could give the little lord that in a story…"

Edward was waving frantically at the laundress from atop the servant's shoulders. "A good night to you, Mistress Gatty! I'm off to bed now…to get warm!"

"You sleep well, little lord. And don't you be dreaming of any wicked sprites, not

Barguests or Fetches or anything else that might be walking abroad on All Hallows."

"A Barguest is a big black dog," said Edward. "I wouldn't be afraid of any dog, Gatty. But what's a Fetch?"

"It's a double," replied the old woman. "It looks just like you and yet isn't you. It is thought to be a token…" she paused, growing reticent and finished lamely, "…a…token of bad things to come. But nought a fair young gentleman like you will ever have to worry about."

It seemed deep melancholy had suddenly overcome Gatty. "I must go, my warm hearth awaits," she mumbled, her former fervour gone. She curtseyed towards the Duke and Duchess, then she was fleeing the churchyard and was soon lost in a haze of smoke.

"It's growing cold…so cold…" Anne shivered and drew her fur-lined mantle close about her shoulders. She looked frail and pallid in the deepening glow of the dying bonfires.

Richard nodded. "Yes, let us wait no longer out here. These children are long past their bed-time"

Surrounded by their followers, with young Edward riding high on the servant's shoulders and Katherine skipping along beside them, chattering gaily, the Duke and Duchess made their way through the streets, littered with deadened turnip lanterns and awash with night-fog and acrid smoke. Most of the town children had departed and only a few old souls who had had too much to drink cloistered around the market cross. "God bless the Duke of Gloucester and our little Lord, Edward of Middleham!" shouted one such inebriated greybeard, raising a mazer on high. Edward waved frantically at him before the ducal party entered the torch-lit maw of the great gatehouse of Middleham Castle.

It was still dark outside. The castle was silent, as much as any great stronghold of its size was silent; mice scuttled inside walls and the winds soughed around the keep and battlements.

Edward sat up in his comfortable bed, clutching the warm coverlet to him, and glanced towards his nurse. She was lying on a truckle bed near the brazier, snoring loudly, her cover pulled over her head.

After he had returned to the castle with his parents and Katherine, Edward had been whisked away, washed, clothed in a bed gown and put to bed with some smelly liniment rubbed on his chest. He had enjoyed the warmth, the feeling of his cold-numbed fingers and toes returning to life, and he had soon fallen asleep.

But he had dreamed, his dreams unlike any he had experienced before. Grinning carved turnips rolling through a fog tinged orange by the bonfires, a hook-nosed, green-jowled witch with her apron full of unripe nuts that she let fall to bounce along the ground…each one had an evil little face, scrunched up and leering. Behind the crone, a white horse was galloping, but it had gills flapping on its neck and a screaming child tangled in its green weedy mane…

Swinging his legs over the edge of the bed, Edward sucked in the air. He felt hot and cold in turns, and that frightening tightness he got in his chest at times began to make its hated presence felt. He hoped he would not start coughing and wake his nurse.

He was going to do something forbidden. He would have to be very quiet, very careful…

Quietly Edward slipped to the oak chest in the corner and pulled out the folded garments within. He hopped crazily on one foot, afraid he would topple over as he struggled with his hose—young boys of high birth did not normally dress themselves. He was not sure exactly *what* he was doing, what compelled him—perhaps his sense of illness, of deep unease; memories of the gurning turnips and smoking fires, the scent of which still clung to his hair, redolent of winter…or the thought of the giant's dog, Wolfshead, his fate lost in time, perhaps still appearing through the mist after his life was extended by the one-eyed wizard…

Heart hammering, he crept to the chamber door, opened it as silently as he could, and slid into the corridor beyond. The torches in their brackets were burning low; no guards patrolled here, for none were needed, in this, the strongest, most safe part of the castle.

On silent feet, Edward descended one staircase and then another, cold tunnels of winding stone where tendrils of chill air drifted up to ruffle his hair. He passed a series of silent doors, went down another broad staircase, and at last reached the door leading out into the bailey. The servants were all abed and the door was bolted for the night; he fumbled at it with his small, thin fingers, fearing he would make a terrible noise and wake everyone nearby…but luck was with him, and the bolt slid back soundlessly. Grasping the door ring, he stumbled out into the night-enshrouded bailey.

To his surprise, the icy air seemed to ease him rather than increase his affliction this time. In the far west, near to setting, the moon rode a sea of shredded cumulus. Cloud-shadows soared across its face, black hags riding high on besoms. Up above, the boar banner of Edward's father snapped and crackled in the wind. The sentries still stood upon walls and gatehouse…he could hear the murmur of their voices, snatches of conversation brought to his ears on the sharp wind. They were about to change positions with their fellows and were glad of it; for those soon to be off duty, the rest of the night would be in a comfortable bed after a mug of heated ale to warm their bellies.

Cloaked in the shadows, Edward slunk towards the grey mass of the gatehouse. He was just a slip of a thing, in his dark blue cloak, the hood drawn up to hide his face and hair. The soldiers above kept on with their banter as they exchanged posts with their fellows. They were not looking for someone trying to get out of the castle, and they weren't much concerned about anyone trying to get in. The curfew bell had long since been rung and the gates were closed although there was a small door on one side, used for foot traffic during the day. It was barred at night but only by a latch. If there was any real danger in the town, the portcullis would drop, protecting the inner ward with hard metal rather than stout wood reinforced with steel bands.

Breathless with his own audacity more than his usual winter affliction, Edward hurried up to the side door and tripped the latch. The sentries' laughter sounded above, ringing loud in the dark stone passageway leading out to the street, hiding any noise the little boy might have made.

Then he was out of the gatehouse, free and running, though the cold wind, rising in intensity, clawed at his lungs, making them hurt with each breath again. Which way, *which way*? It seemed the whole world was opening up to him on this strange, smoky night.

His gaze locked on the road that wound up the hill toward Coverham, where the monks dwelt in a fine stone priory and the bones of some of Edward's Neville ancestors lay enclosed in stone tomb chests, silently dreaming into eternity within the darkened church nave. This was the road that could lead to adventure...or doom. Once before, long ago, he'd had an unwelcome adventure, following a strange old woman into a winter's snowstorm...but this felt different, *was* different. He was younger then and had been tricked by the woman into leaving the safety of the castle...now he moved of his own choice, his own desire. And it felt good.

He set one foot upon the rutted track, tentative, knowing how angry his father would be if he knew what he was doing His mother's anguish bothered him even more—in his mind's eye he could envision her distressed face—but with an effort, he forced such visions away. He would not stay out long, would not do anything *too* rash. He only wanted to clear his mind of nightmares—and, for a short while, wander free as if he were the son of some humble cottager, away from nurses and tutors, from bowing servants and the unbreakable daily rituals of a noble household. Free to tumble on the floor with puppies, to wear mud-stained hose, to sport a rip in his shirt, to walk about with his hair tangled like a bird's nest. Free to wander alone in the dark on haunted All Hallow's Eve.

Behind him, in the town's heart, the bell of St Alkelda's was still tolling, though its peals had slowed, growing more sombre and doom-laden. The trees on the roadside swayed, skeletal arms scraping at the stars; a cat as black as soot ran out of them, staring at Edward with large, luminous green eyes before darting between the nearest cottages. Night-fog now fully displaced the earlier smoke, rolling in thick grey clouds down the expanse of the road, moving almost as if it were a living creature.

Edward began to run towards it, facing the fog bank as if he were a hero about to engage a dragon. Just up to the hilltop; he would stop there and go no further. From the height, he would look down upon the place where he would one day be lord, even if the mist shrouded it he knew it was there—the mighty stone castle, the brewery and bakehouse, the mews, kennels and stables, and beyond Middleham town with its two crosses, broad market square, Saint Alkelda's and the holy well… A shudder gripped him though, even as he thought of his future as a future duke and great magnate. When that day finally came, his father would be dead…

Thrusting that awful, unsettling thought aside, Edward struggled on through the roiling vapours that cloaked the road. On his left he could just see the dark hump of William's Hill, the forerunner of Middleham Castle, built after the conquest by Ribald Rufus. Rabbits and badgers dwelt there now rather than Norman lords, and old coins and rusted horse harness came out of their warrens and setts, coveted by the local children who played there. Edward himself had found an old brooch there once, a prized treasure …but he dared not go there on this night of all nights. Who knows what lurked within the trees that sprouted from that earthen motte?

He reached the foot of the rise at the top of the road and continued up it, puffing. Reaching the summit, he turned around to survey the land around him. Below, to his delight, he was able to see Middleham Castle, the fire braziers on the walls glowing dully through the mist. The town beyond, though, was almost completely obliterated; the top of the church stuck up from the murk, a craggy finger pointing towards heaven. Its bells were muffled, dreary.

Edward turned to look at what lay on the other side of the road. It was too far to see Coverham even on a clear day, but he heard the vaguest trace of the monks' tolling all-night bells.

And then he heard something else, something unexpected…hooves upon the road. Creaking wheels. Chanting.

Panic gripped him and he dived into a nearby bush. Its limbs tore at him, poked his face, tangled in his hair. He nearly cried out as red jewels of blood appeared on the back of his hand but managed to hold his cry back.

Out of the fog-bank covering the road trundled a covered wagon drawn by two raven-black horses. Surrounding it were six cowled figures, their faces hidden by their voluminous hoods. Six candles burned upon the cart, green and eerie as the 'corpse-candles' that flitted over bogs. The figures chanted in low, dreary voices:

This ae night, this ae night,
Every night and all,
Fire and fleet and candle-light,
And Christ receive thy soul...

Edward realised then he gazed upon a funeral procession. Perhaps it had come from Coverham? Whoever had died must have been a great person, because the funeral wain's cover was painted with sumptuous designs and heavily gilded.

Suddenly the cowled figures halted in their tracks. None looked up or to the side but they had stopped right beside the bush where Edward hid, as if they knew of his presence. He wanted to remain hidden, but yet he knew...to hide was the coward's way. A knight was always brave...his father was always brave.

Hesitantly he crept from the bush and stood beside the funeral cortege. The cowled heads did not move. He saw no hint of breath in the air—before his own mouth there were puffs of white. "Who are you?" he breathed. "What are you doing here?"

No answer...but one monk's arm, wrapped in its long black sleeve, moved. A waxen-pale hand pointed into the chariot, at its hidden contents.

Edward teetered forward, repelled yet somehow drawn to the death-carriage too. This was a dream…surely it must be a dream!

Reaching the back of the wagon, he drew a long, scarlet velvet cloth aside and stared at a coffin. Before his horrified eyes, the lid lifted and its occupant sat up, staring straight at him.

It was a young boy as pallid as moonlight with no colour in lips or cheeks, even his hair like cobwebs. But the face…the face. Although drained of any colour he knew that face…*for it was his own*!

"W-ho who are you?" Edward stammered.

The boy smiled, his mouth curving up in a black slash; not a pleasant or welcoming smile. He spoke then, though Edward did not see his lips move, "You know who I am and what I am. Gatty knew. I am your Fetch…"

Edward stared at the other boy, his mirror-image save for his pallor and for his eyes—they were wide and staring with irises so large they appeared black instead of blue-grey. His knees went weak and he began to tremble…

"Don't be afraid, Edward," said the Fetch, holding out his thin white arms as if wanting to embrace him. "You're not afraid of yourself, are you? Soon we'll be together, always…"

Edward gave a strangled yell and leapt back from the rear of the funeral chariot as if he'd been burnt. Skidding on wet, dank leaves, he veered down the hill towards his father's castle. Once or twice, he cast a hasty glance over his shoulder to see if the Fetch or the cowled monks pursued him, but the mist had grown even more thick and cloying and he could not tell. On the final time he dared look back, he lost his balance and fell into an icy puddle on the roadside, skinning his knees on the stones hidden by the shallow water.

Sobbing in fear, his lungs on fire, he picked himself up and continued on his mad run for safety.

After what seemed an eternity, he reached the castle gatehouse and dived for the small door through which he had escaped. Clutching the door-ring, he yanked on it. Nothing happened. Cold iron burned into his palm. One of the guards must have realised it was unlocked and replaced the inside latch.

"No, no!" he began to shout between wheezes, hammering on the door as hard as he could with his fists.

He fell to his knees, his pounding lessening. Black spots danced in his vision as barking coughs broke from his lips.

And then he heard voices from the other side of the door, and suddenly his tear-filled eyes were dazzled by the light of many torches…

He woke in his bed, warm and familiar. Grey November light flooded through the window. He felt weak and bruised…but it was day and he was alive.

Over in the corner, his nurse Annie rose from her stool. "God be praised you are awake at last!"

He blinked at her, rubbed his eyes. "It is morning. I am awake. What is so praiseworthy about that, nurse?!

"Dear young lord." Tears were on her cheeks. "It's been a full day. You were found outside the gate on All Hallow's Eve, in some kind of a faint. It's all my fault too, I should have heard you leave and realised you had slipped out…"

"No, no, it's not your fault," the boy said stoutly. "All blame lies with me alone. If my sire is angry with you, I will beg him to turn his anger on me instead, for I have been the pro—prodigal son. I think that's what they call it in the Bible."

Annie laughed then, wiping away her tears. "You have an old head for a little lad, sometimes," she said, heading for the door. "Now I will go and summon the Duke and Duchess. They have been beside themselves with fear."

Richard and Anne sat by their son's bed, listening with solemn faces as Edward apologised for his ill-advised wandering and begged their forgiveness.

"You knew the cold night air was harmful to you," said Anne, her face showing signs of the strain she had been under. "And that you might have been abducted or worse by any rogue passing on the road. Why, oh why did you behave so foolishly, Edward?"

Edward hung his head, his fairish hair falling over his face. "I should have known better but…"

"But what?" asked Richard. "Speak freely, child."

"I wanted to be brave and bold...out there alone," Edward said, lifting his chin, his look suddenly tinged with defiance. "By my age, Father, you had been taken with Grandmere Cecily as a prisoner of the Lancastrians and then you were sent away to Burgundy for safety with your brother George."

"Your time will come," said Richard firmly, his voice a little softer. "I promise you that, Edward. But *you* must promise to be mindful of your health. You will not remember it, but we had to call the physic to you after we found you at the gate. You fell down senseless..."

Edward bit his lip, ashamed...but yet still doubt burned with him. "Father," he said in a hoarse whisper, "will I...will I really be like other boys?"

"Of course you will. Why wouldn't you? As I told you before, I was not a strong child either. I outgrew my maladies."

"But Father..." Edward's voice sank even lower. "I-I saw the Fetch. There on the road to Coverham. It looked just like me. That means I..."

"It means exactly *nothing,*" said Richard vehemently. "And you saw *nothing.* The Fetch is an old wife's tale, and you were either dreaming...or delirious. Some folk are known to walk when asleep; perhaps that is what happened to you. Now..." He rose and pushed Edward gently back against the bolster, drawing up the quilt with its embroidery of hounds and boars. "I bid you rest. The physic said you must not exert yourself for a few days."

The Duke made to leave the chamber but as he did, there was a flurry of wings at the window, momentarily blocking the hazy light and making the room grow dim as night.

Anne gasped, hand fluttering to her throat in alarm, while Richard sprinted to the window and stared out. "It's gone, whatever it was."

"A black bird, an ill omen," murmured Anne, face bleak.

"Don't *you* start, wife," said Richard. "It's clear where the boy gets it from. Come..." He drew the shutters. "Let us leave our son to rest."

But despite his confident words, the Duke of Gloucester halted just outside Edward's chamber door, after waiting for

Anne to leave for her solar and the company of her ladies.

Head bowed, he murmured a prayer of protection he remembered from the Psalms, *"God is my refuge and my fortress, in whom I trust. Surely he will save you from the fowler's snare and from the deadly pestilence. He will cover you with his feathers, and under his wings you will find refuge..."*

His voice trailed away, suddenly grown thick, and he crossed himself ardently.

Outside, the bells of St Alkelda's began to toll, summoning the townsfolk to Mass—it was November 2, All Soul's Day, when the *Dies Irae* was chanted and ancestors' graves decorated with gifts and offerings. There were sounds of life, carts creaking, dogs barking, men and women shouting greetings.

And somewhere, in the far distance, a chorus of unfamiliar voices sang a strange and somehow sinister old song—

> *This ae night, this ae night,*
> *Every night and all,*
> *Fire and fleet and candle-light,*
> *And Christ receive thy soul.*

THE END

Author's Notes-

Halloween has always been my favourite holiday. Although it was not celebrated in quite the same way we do today, it was still a special time in the Middle Ages and held some traces of older practices from a far distant past.

Of course, there were no pumpkins in medieval England—it was carved turnips that were used till fairly recent times. Much harder to carve…but also much more sinister and far spookier looking!

Souling was a real tradition instead of 'trick or treat'. You can still get some very good online recipes for Soul Cakes.

I have a lifelong interest in British and Irish folklore and that was my real basis for writing this story, alongside my love of Halloween. The three stories told to the town's children by Gatty are my versions of authentic tales from the Yorkshire Dales. Water Horses are interesting as they are more commonly found in Scotland and Ireland—perhaps they are an old Celtic remnant? The name of Penhill, the home of the unfriendly giant, certainly is half-Celtic—'Pen' means 'head' and it is frequently used for a hill or high place. However, the giant himself is definitely Norse in character and legend says he descended from the thunder-god Thor. In the original story his name was unknown so I called him by the name of another Yorkshire giant (Yorkshire seems to have many fearsome giants!)

The haunting poem that appears twice is the Lyke-Wake Dirge, an old traditional song—difficult to date but before the 16th c, possibly as early as the 14th c.

J.P. Reedman, October 15, 2023

OTHER BOOKS BY J.P. REEDMAN:

RICHARD III and the WARS OF THE ROSES

I, RICHARD PLANTAGENET: THE PREQUELS. Richard's childhood and youth. 3 books

I, RICHARD PLANTAGENET. 3 book series. First two are Richard's life from Barnet to Bosworth; the third is a tie-in about Henry Stafford, the treacherous Duke of Buckingham.

BLOOD OF ROSES and SECRET MARRIAGES—Edward IV's battle for the throne and his tangled love life!

MEDIEVAL BABES—series of novels on lesser-known medieval women. Eleanor of Provence, Rosamund Clifford, Eleanor of Brittany, Katherine, illegitimate daughter of Richard III, Mary of Woodstock the Merry Nun, Juliane illegitimate daughter of Henry I, Mabel de Belleme the poisoner, Countess Ela of Salisbury, The Other Margaret Beaufort (mother of Henry Stafford), Dangereuse the grandmother of Eleanor of Aquitaine, and Matilda, wife of Henry I

ROBIN HOOD:

The Hood Game-3 book series set in a Sherwood full of myth and magic.

THE STONEHENGE SAGA—A novel of the Bronze Age incorporating the Arthurian myths.

AND MANY MORE!

UK AMAZON LINK TO AUTHOR PAGE: https://www.amazon.co.uk/J-P-Reedman/e/B009UTHBUE

USA AMAZON LINK TO AUTHOR PAGE:
https://www.amazon.com/stores/J.P.Reedman/author/B009UTBUE

Printed in Great Britain
by Amazon